Sun & Moon SISTERS

Written and Illustrated by **Khoa Le**

INSIGHT KIDS

San Rafael, California

Sun and Moon were sisters.
They ruled the sky together.

But sometimes they were jealous of one another.

They often asked each other:

"Which one of us is more important?"

"Which one of us do the people
love the most?"

One day they decided
to switch roles.
Sun would do Moon's
job and Moon would
do Sun's job.

That night, instead of going to
bed as usual, Sun stayed up late
and took Moon's place.

In the middle of the night, Sun was still shining. After a long day, everyone wanted to rest, but nobody could close their eyes in the bright light.

Hot and exhausted, the girls and boys called to the sky,
"Moon, dear Moon, where are you?
Come back home; let Sun go to sleep."

But Sun still kept shining.
Plants and flowers wilted
from the heat. The bright
green colors that Sun loved
so much turned a limp brown.

A worried Sun said to Moon,
"I give up. Please take command
over the sky again."

So Moon reappeared and
sprinkled the sky with stars
like magic.

Moon's silver light soothed
everybody into a gentle deep sleep.

The next morning, the sky was still dark,
because Moon was still hovering in the air.
There was no Sun to warm the earth,
and everything felt gloomy.

The humans were cold,
the animals hibernated, and the land
turned dark. Trees shed their leaves
as if winter was coming.

Sun and Moon were confused.

"So, which one of us is needed most?"

"You are both important," shouted the children.
"Don't envy each other anymore.
Please get back to work just like you used to."

From then on, Sun brightened
the sky, all day long.

Kids could run free in the fields
and bathe in the warm sunlight.

At night, Moon would rise and gently
stroke the earth with her silver magic.

Sun and Moon have been loving sisters ever since.

KHOA LE is an illustrator, graphic designer, painter, and writer. She graduated from the Fine Arts University in Ho Chi Minh City. She has published thirteen books, seven of which she both wrote and illustrated. Her artwork has been featured in numerous exhibitions in Vietnam, Hong Kong, Singapore, and Korea.

INSIGHT
KIDS

PO Box 3088
San Rafael, CA 94912
www.insighteditions.com

Find us on Facebook: www.facebook.com/InsightEditions
Follow us on Twitter: @insighteditions

First published in the United States in 2016 by Insight Kids,
an imprint of Insight Editions.
Originally published in French in Switzerland in 2014 by NuiNui.
Copyright © 2014 by Snake SA.
English translation © 2016 by Snake SA.

NuiNui ® is a registered trademark and registered by Snake SA.

nuinui

Chemin du Tsan Péri 10
3971 Chermignon
Switzerland

Library of Congress Cataloging-in-Publication Data available.

ISBN: 978-1-60887-732-4

ROOTS of PEACE   REPLANTED PAPER

Insight Editions, in association with Roots of Peace, will plant two trees for each tree
used in the manufacturing of this book. Roots of Peace is an internationally renowned
humanitarian organization dedicated to eradicating land mines worldwide and
converting war-torn lands into productive farms and wildlife habitats. Roots of Peace
will plant two million fruit and nut trees in Afghanistan and provide farmers there
with the skills and support necessary for sustainable land use.

Manufactured in Shaoguan, China, by Insight Editions

201610R0

10 9 8 7 6 5 4 3 2